# The Veteran and The Boy

Stephen P. Smith

*By Stephen P. Smith*

### Fiction

The Unsound Convictions of Judge
Stephen Mentall

The Veteran and The Boy

### Computer Science

Thinking About Computer Programming?

### Biography

The Charlie Chaplin Walk

First Published 2018

ISBN: 978-1-7292842-3-0

# 1

There were two things the talk of Devizes Market Place at four o'clock on that Tuesday afternoon.

It wasn't market day so the price of things was not discussed.

Nor was the weather – the sky was clear and there was no wind. The shops, a mixture of redbrick and stone, were busy and the smell of the brewery hung over the town, but the locals were used to that so nobody thought to mention it.

The coal merchant's steam lorry puffed its way through, but they'd run it for years and the black hessian sacks of coal, propped on its flatbed, and the

men with their caps, dirty faces
(some stern, some cheeky) and
brown leather flak jackets, were an
everyday sight too.

The fishmongers, with its red
canvas canopy, dulled by the sun,
had fresh stock and a pig hung in
the butcher's plate-glass window.
The greengrocer, wearing his khaki
shopkeeper's coat, weighed out
apples and tipped them into brown
paper bags.

The agent's office, next to
the cinema, advertised the land
that was for sale, what it was good
for and whether it was tenanted.
But there was always land for sale
so the window only attracted those
looking to buy or those who were
just plain curious and liked to keep

up with these things.

As for the Veteran he stood in front of the ladies window of Sloper's Drapery Store admiring the mannequins as they were stripped and dressed. It was the same every Tuesday. He gathered comment, the usual comments of disgust and suspicion, and was one of the two things that were the talk of the market place on that Tuesday afternoon. And the other? Just about anybody that was not talking about the Veteran was talking about the shiny new school bus parked in the middle of the market place.

\*

Billy Shelton liked the new bus, liked its dark green paint, large black tyres with white hubs, radiator and the ever present starting-handle. The number plate was AM1921, and 1921 was the year of his birth: a simple connection that made him feel special. He pulled a pencil and a blue clothbound notebook from his trouser pocket and added AM1921 to a long list of numbers he'd collected. When something bad happened his father would ask him for the numbers he'd seen, when he'd seen them and who was about at the time. And when Mike Hillier, a sandy-haired boy with sharp, piercing blue eyes, found out he would clip Billy's ear for being a policeman's snitch.

And on this Tuesday afternoon, when the shop assistants had finished dressing the mannequins in their new outfits, the Veteran turned and shuffled towards the children. His gait was so strange they always stopped whatever they were doing when he hobbled by: a conker fight would cease, the brown chestnuts left to swing on bits of string in the breeze; the trade of a dead frog for a tuppenth of boiled sweets; the reassembly of a bicycle chain and the skimming of a pebble on a dew pond hung as if an artist had painted them.

Billy was glad that no car backfired today, and no fork of

lightning lit the sky as these would cause the Veteran to cower and his strange mumblings to become frantic cries. Then the children would laugh and jeer, but none was brave enough to go near him. And Billy would look on the man, wondering about his past and whether he felt as alone as he did.

Nobody was sure where the Veteran slept at night, but the rumour was he bedded down in hedgerows in the summer, and barns in the winter. Billy sometimes saw him in Market Lavington, the village where he lived. Sometimes he saw him up on the plain – a large area of flat land above his village.  But more often he was seen here in the main town,

Devizes.

When Billy asked his father about the Veteran, all he would say was, "The war affected him." But he never added any more to his pleas of, "What war? What happened? Was he blown up?" other than to warn him to stay clear of him.

Mike Hillier had once announced, "It was the Great War and he'd been taken prisoner and tortured by the Germans." And then some older boys beat him up for being a know-all and he, in turn, beat up Billy Shelton for simply being Billy Shelton.

He watched Paul Redshaw, a boy who lived in the town but hung around with Hillier, load a peashooter and catch the Veteran on the cheek then laugh as he flapped and attacked the air. Mike Hillier gathered some small stones from the gutter then peppered the Veteran's greatcoat. He jeered as the Veteran jumped.

Billy looked towards the bus, hoping the driver would open the doors and call the children to board. But there was no sign of the doors being opened, instead the driver sat at his steering wheel and turned the pages of a newspaper.

"Leave him be," yelled Billy.

Redshaw turned towards him, his face full of threat. "You what?"

Billy stared into Redshaw's dark black eyes. There was menace in them and he wished he'd said nothing. He wished he'd walked around the market place again, or hidden behind the market cross, to chew the time up and avoid the rage of the bullies between the school bell and the driver opening the doors to the bus.

"What did you say?" asked Redshaw, flicking back his dark hair and pressing his face into Billy's.

"Shelton's got a friend," jeered Hillier.

"He's your friend now is he?" asked Redshaw.

Billy's legs felt heavy and he trembled.

"Shelton's got a friend," chanted the other boys. The other

boys always joined in the jibes, but never the hitting.

He felt Redshaw grab hold of his ear and twist, a hot burning feeling rode up his head. He didn't really see what happened next: the Veteran had somehow waded towards Redshaw and now, with his stick flailing, struck the bully across the side of his head. The boys backed away as the Veteran attacked the air, keeping Hillier and Redshaw at bay like a lion tamer at a circus. With each protest the Veteran jabbed his stick, and Billy rubbed his ear.

The driver unlocked and opened the doors to the bus. "You," he yelled, pointing at the Veteran, "Clear off."

The Veteran stared and appeared to shake his head, but it was more of a tremble than a shake. He backed away and only then did the driver beckon the children towards the bus.

The boys allowed the girls to board first. They always did – it was a rule of the driver. Then they jostled and shoved and took up their seats as Redshaw ran along the outside of the bus, yelling at Billy that he was going to get him tomorrow.

Billy took a seat but Mike Hillier dragged him out and shoved him towards the back. He sat on the boards of the gangway, still rubbing his ear and patted his pocket to make sure he'd not lost the shopping list which his mother had given him that morning. He dreaded losing his mother's list, dreaded any incident that might unleash her anger and dreaded getting off the bus where Hillier was sure to punch and kick him.

As the bus pulled away he listened to the roar of the engine, the whine of the straight cut gearbox and guessed when the driver would change gear. The gear changes were smooth, sending a slight rumble below the deck. The old bus used to lurch and the driver held back for as a long as he could until the engine screamed or laboured for a different cog. He listened to other boys list the new bus's virtues, the size of the engine, its top speed (if only it were unleashed) and Billy felt peeved the girls were learning about the bus from somebody other than him.

At a small village at the foot of a steep hill the bus pulled up and half a dozen boys and two girls alighted.  Billy parked himself on one of the hard brown leather seats set in a chrome frame. He watched an elderly man look upon the new bus, and Billy now felt important to be on that bus.

The next stop was at Black Dog Farm (where a friend of the driver's hitched a ride) before it trundled along the lanes and came to its final stop outside the church in Market Lavington. As soon as the doors opened Billy dashed off to get ahead of Mike Hillier, to disappear before he got a final cuff of the day. Hillier's mother and sister, Molly, were waiting for him. Billy was safe, the tension sank and even Molly smiled, through her freckles, as if somehow she knew she'd saved him. She had long, dark locks and always wore a white dress with a red bow. Molly was a pretty girl, and her mother would beam with pride whenever anybody mentioned it.

*

Nettleton's store was deep and narrow. The shelves behind the long counter were painted green and the produce was arranged in its neat alcoves. A wooden crate of apples, parked beside the scales, filled the shop with a sweet smell. Billy waited his turn and scuffed his shoes across the diamond patterned black and white floor.

Mr Nettleton always looked taller in the shop for the space behind the counter was raised so he could keep a good eye on his customers. Two women, who Billy knew from the church, queued before him, gossiping. They had stout faces, wore old woollen coats and their conversations complained about the vicar, the schoolmistress and the prices in Nettleton's store. But, when it came time to serve them, Mr Nettleton ignored their chatter as these old women were well known for their wounding remarks.

When they had filled their wicker baskets, handed over their coins and made to leave, Mr Nettleton turned towards Billy. "Have you got a list for me?"

Billy nodded, and Mr Nettleton wiped his hands on his white coat, raised his half-moon glasses from a chain around his neck and took the list. "We're out of bread," he announced, placing the list down on the counter.

Billy watched his smooth hands cut some cheese and pour sugar into a paper bag. A light bulb, hanging by its own wire, shone on his bald head.

"On your mother's

account?" he asked.

Billy nodded, took the cheese and sugar and stopped at the doorway to check all was clear. He wasn't ready to face his mother, wasn't ready to explain the lack of bread: instead he hurried up a lane and across fields to see his uncle Joe. Farmhands, in gumboots old shirts and braces, were working the fields, but none stopped, none looked up and none bothered him.

Uncle Joe worked at a railway station on the road south of Black Dog Farm. The station was simply known as Lavington Station: Billy minded this and he would plot and dream it would be moved closer to his village and be renamed Market Lavington

Station. But he kept this to himself because he was often ridiculed when he shared his thoughts. Uncle Joe would not ridicule him. But Uncle Joe's cottage was alongside the station, and Billy didn't want him to think he might have to move.

The station was a grand building, almost as grand as the one in Devizes; though Devizes had a tunnel which Billy envied. But his father said the goods yard was important and Billy was pleased that his uncle Joe, who worked there, had an important job.

Billy unhooked a white painted gate and let himself onto the platform with an over bridge, waiting rooms and offices. He jumped onto the platform weighing scales and watched the needle flick up and settle.

"Be wanting to post yourself away or summit, young Billy?" asked the station master, a thin man with a large nose and a hook for a right hand. "I dares say we could parcel thee up." He then chuckled at his own joke; he always made a joke when Billy arrived. "Yer uncle Joe's up the goods yard."

Billy ran over and got a wave from the man in the signal box. He found Uncle Joe shovelling coal into a waggon, hooked up to a shunter.

"Hello Billy," he said,

straightening himself up and throwing his shovel on to the heap of coal. "I'm off to Patney in a bit. Do you wanna ride?"

Billy nodded and smiled. He never said much to Uncle Joe and Uncle Joe rarely said much back.

Uncle Joe adjusted his black cap which sat on his head of thick, black hair. He lifted Billy onto the footplate and then followed him up into the cab.

Patney was the next station down the line and he only got to go there when Uncle Joe drove the train. And that only happened when Stan Smith had the day off.

The engine quietly hissed out steam, and Billy felt the draught of hot air from the firebox.

He tucked the sugar and cheese carefully between his feet, afraid of his mother's anger, should anything happen to them.

Uncle Joe gave him a smile, before patting down his blue overalls and winding a brass handle with his blackened hands.

The shunter chugged forward, the coupling pulled tight and the coal waggon gave a deep clanking groan as it followed on behind.

"'e's not set the points," said Uncle Joe and, as they approached the mainline, he leaned out the cab and yelled, "Doug, set the points." Billy watched some metal rods pull tight and the rails move across in front of them.

Uncle Joe wound the handle again and the shunter moved out onto the mainline. He then shovelled some more coal into the firebox and pushed its door shut with the tip of his boot. "That should be enough to get us there."

Billy gazed out across the countryside where oak trees peppered the hedgerows and sheaves of hay stood like miniature wigwams. The train passed into one of the many cuttings and the noise of the engine echoed off the earth banks. Although Billy felt safe in the shunter, where nobody could make nasty comments or beat him up, he felt even safer in the cuttings where nobody could see him.

The burning coal smelt like the fire at home, but the heat, radiating from the cast-iron bulkhead, was more intense and Billy's head felt hot and beads of sweat ran down his forehead.

A distant mournful whistle sounded.

"Express train's coming. 'old on," said Uncle Joe. "'e's coming through Patney now."

As the noise of the Express grew Billy felt flutters of excitement grow in his stomach. A column of steam turreted above a bend in the track. The rails tingled and sung as the train bore down. A crescendo of noise, then whoosh as the passing train blasted their cab. The clickety-clack faded into the distance and the smell of burning clinker hung in the air.

The shunter glided into the siding at Patney, Uncle Joe turned some wheels and the engine came to a stop and let out a long hiss of steam. Another man, short in stature but broad across the shoulders, came to help, and the two men shovelled out the coal into concrete bins set in an earth bank.

A light breeze blew along the platform and carried with it a dab of rain. Billy watched the station clock as the two men finished their work then settled into a conversation. They took it in turns to speak and nodded in agreement at everything that was said. The afternoon was now passing by and he feared he'd be in trouble for being late home. He willed them to finish talking, but it was past five o'clock before the distance between the men subtly grew and Billy knew their conversation was coming to an end.

With a final wave goodbye Uncle Joe climbed back aboard, turned some more wheels and, following a deep throb from the engine, they shunted back onto the mainline.

After a few minutes, Uncle Joe announced, "I'll let you out by West Park Farm." Billy felt relieved; from the farm he could take a shortcut home.

The shunter slowed to a

walking pace, Billy grabbed his sugar and cheese and jumped from the cab. Uncle Joe called after him to hop over the fence and be sure not to play on the railway's property. Billy scrambled up the embankment, using the entrances to the rabbit burrows as footholds, before running across the fields to home.

The kitchen door was unlocked, but his mother was out. He left the cheese and sugar on the dresser next to a pot where his mother kept the housekeeping money. He then opened a stripped wood door and clunked up the bare staircase to his bedroom and lay on his bed watching the light through the trees trace shadows across the ceiling.

He heard his mother return and, with his legs tingling in apprehension, got up and checked his door was closed then lay back down on his bed. He listened to her moving around in the kitchen, listened to it go quiet and then listened to the door at the bottom of the stairs open.

"You're a very wicked boy," she shouted, her voice quivering with anger.

He drew his legs to his stomach as his mother's words leapt up the stairs. He closed his eyes and tried to think what he might have done wrong this time.

"Come down 'ere," she demanded.

She met him by the door at the foot of the stairs. Her dark eyes dug into him and her chin trembled with fury.

She raised an index finger. "I asked you to do one small thing. One small thing," she said, wagging the finger. "I work my fingers to the bone for you and your father and do you ever lift a finger to help? Out playing with your friends, daydreaming in your bedroom, never a thought for anybody but yourself."

Billy thought of his non-existent friends and longed for his bedroom.

"What am I going to get your father for his tea?"

"I don't know."

"Don't know. You're right you don't know. Not bread that's for sure." Her lips quivered and her eyes grew darker.

Now Billy knew what her anger was about. "They didn't have any," he began.

"Don't you lie to me."

"They didn't."

"They had the sugar and the cheese. Who's ever heard of a shop that sells sugar and cheese but not bread?"

"Nettleton's," replied Billy.

"Don't you answer me back, my boy."

"They'd run out," protested Billy, but he knew his mother would never believe him.

"I ask you to get three simple

things and you can't even do that. Where's the list I gave you?"

"Mr Nettleton kept it."

"You lost it more like. Get back up to your room and keep out of my sight until I call you down for supper. I don't know what your father's going to say."

\*

Billy sat at the kitchen table and watched his father greet his mother as he did every evening with neither an embrace nor a kiss.

He hung his tunic on a peg and undid the top button of his blue shirt and loosened his tie allowing his thick neck to roll out. Peering into the centre of a worn, oval mirror which hung above the washstand, he patted down his mass of shiny black hair that swept back from an even line across his forehead.

Leaning over the washstand he lapped water across his thickset face. He then reached down and grasped the white cloth that hung on a single metal arm of a towel rail. He wiped his brow, mopped his face, then folded and replaced the dirty cloth.

He crossed to the table, took his seat and removed his police epaulettes. Billy dreaded the question. But he knew he'd be asked it. Billy waited. His father picked up his knife and fork and speared a slice of ham and a pickle.

"You were in the market place this afternoon?"

It sounded like being in the market place was a sin.

"Did you see the Veteran?"

Billy nodded.

"Jack Hillier said the Veteran hit that Redshaw boy."

"Only because Paul Redshaw hit me."

"Don't lie to your father," said Billy's mother.

"I ain't lying," Billy protested.

"What did Redshaw hit you for?" asked his father.

"He just does."

"He must have had a reason. Did you hit him first?"

"No."

"Then he wouldn't have hit you. You stay away from that Veteran and don't make excuses for him."

"I ain't."

"Something needs to be done about him," said his mother. "Can't have him going around hitting the children."

His father's eyes suddenly scanned the table. "Why's there no bread?"

"You've got something to say to your father haven't you?" said his mother.

"No," replied Billy.

His mother's face, edged by her long brown hair, darkened and her eyes flitted wildly as Billy's stomach filled with hot needles of fear.

"What are you going to say to your father?"

Billy dipped his head and worried his right big toe into the flagstone floor as if to drill a hole. "Nothing."

"You'll go straight to your room if you don't own up."

"I didn't bring any bread," said Billy.

"I sent him to school with a list so he could go to Nettleton's on his way home and he comes back with nothing."

"I got the cheese," protested Billy, "and the sugar."

"Don't contradict," replied his mother.

"Do as your mother tells

you," added his father.

"I did, they didn't have bread."

"Nettleton's always has bread," said his father. "I was in there yesterday and they had plenty."

Billy wolfed down his supper, not looking up until he'd packed his face and swallowed the last morsel.

"You can go to your room now," said his father.

Billy made his way upstairs and flopped onto his bed. He felt his breathing grow shallow and his chest tighten.

## 2

Billy gripped the dresser and edged towards the breakfast table.

"What's the matter with you?" asked his mother.

"Nothing," Billy panted.

"You haven't got your asthma again, have you?" Her voice was challenging.

Billy was silent and fixed his gaze on the mirror above the china sink.

"We can't afford you being sick again, your father's not finished paying the doctor for your last lot of bills. And I don't want you around here all day."

Billy dropped into his chair and let out a short breath.

"*Don't* you sigh at me. Now eat up your breakfast and get ready for school."

Billy pulled the plate towards him and took a tiny bite of sausage.

"Lost your appetite too?"

Billy listened to his chest wheeze as he tried to breathe in. He ate part of the sausage before rasping for another breath. He longed to be well and longed for his mother not to be cross with him.

"You'll make yourself late," she said.

Billy chewed through his meal the best he could before he got up to leave.

"And don't forget to salute your grandfather."

Billy paused by the dresser, raised his right hand to his ear and looked at the man in the photograph. His grandfather, wearing a flat army cap, military tunic and stockinged lower legs that looked like bandages, gazed back. Billy had never met his grandfather, and whenever his mother claimed he'd died bravely for his country he had felt responsible for her loss.

Making his way to the bus he walked until he was out of sight then buckled and gasped as he took rapid short breaths.

He heard the bus before he saw the bus. It came towards him and passed him by, he waved but the driver did not stop. The driver never stopped for late boys. He wiped the welling tears from his eyes and followed the smell of the bus until he got onto the road to the plain. He'd done this before, spent a day up on the plain. The army patrolled it, so there was no need for his father to go up there. The soldiers never bothered him.

The day was muggy, haze hung in the air and whatever breeze there was carried wheat chaff and dust. The chalk road was rutted, and Billy stooped and scuffed up dust and rested often – bent forward, with his hands on his thighs, each breath being pushed back by the weight in his chest.

Ahead the broad-shouldered Reg Quinnell, Mike Hillier's uncle, laboured up the hill. A sack lay across his shoulders and his arms were buckled back with a hand on its top and tail. Quinnell did not rest, did not look back and Billy was relieved for Quinnell and his father were friends.

At the top, where the road made a cross, a sentry box with a soldier stood stiff and impassive. A white wooden sign, with black lettering, said not to venture onto the road crossing the military land. Billy forked left onto a track that ran, like a white scar, along the edge of the plain. Looking down the steep slope, which led to the flatlands below, he picked out the buildings he recognised and watched the men working the fields. He caught the hiss and puff of a train making its way between Lavington and Patney: he wondered if Uncle Joe was stoking the firebox.

Billy walked slowly, he couldn't manage more than a few yards at a time before his legs began to ache, and he had to stop and take in short rasps of air.

As the escarpment levelled out wild gorse bushes gave way to fields. A Fordson tractor worked the land, its engine throbbed and pumped out smoke from its upright exhaust.

A voice from somewhere in front of him spoke. "They've had that thing a twelve month."

Billy felt the thud of his

heartbeat in his head. He'd not seen the old woman approach. Her face was leathery brown and full of lines. He didn't know her, he hoped she didn't know him. She wore a blue headscarf, a threadbare overcoat and carried a basket of eggs.

"Does the job of a dozen or more men and those men are on the parish now, and the man at the wheel used to work with those men and talk with them. It's nay job for a man to work alone and nay life for a man to be without work."

He nodded because he thought he should nod and she went on her way.

The fenced land to his right, on which the soldiers exercised, began to drop away with rolling folds of grassland. He turned off the track towards a dew pond that was hidden in a clump of trees: he knew he could sit unnoticed and scoop up water whenever he fancied. No boys would be there today, none to torment him, none to demand their permission to play or swim, and none to cuff him or throw stones and laugh as he leaped out of their way.

Tiny flies bopped above the water in patches of sunlight that the trees allowed to fall through onto the pond. Water boatmen skimmed the surface and a dragonfly beat its wings and went lazily about its business.

Something unseen made a

plop in the water and left ever
widening rings that lapped the
shore and disturbed a bluebottle
that had rested on the sandy soil of
the water's edge.

The birds chirped and
chattered as a light breeze swayed
the trees. Billy sat with his back
against a leaning oak and closed
his eyes. He took short breaths and
wished himself to be well when he
awoke.

\*

Billy stirred to heavy drops of rain
striking the leaves of the trees
around the dew pond. A few made
their way through and splashed his
face. Between the trees the rain

48

hung in the sky like strands of dark cotton against a grey backdrop. Distant thunder rumbled, and across the dew pond a figure staggered, swayed and twitched towards the water's edge.

As best he could Billy called out, "Veteran, Veteran," to warn him away from the water. But the man did not turn or look across. Instead he stumbled along the dew pond until a fork of lightning, followed by a thunder crack, slumped him to the ground. He then covered his head, quivered and twisted as flashes lit the sky and the thunder cracked with its sharp roars.

Billy willed the storm to pass. Remembering his father's words not to be in the open or under a tree, he shifted towards the water's edge. The Veteran tried to stand but his twitching body dragged him back down.

The thunder became distant, the lightning flashes less intense and the rain peppered the water. He felt his chest tighten and he took sharp breaths. The Veteran managed to stand and wave his arms before stumbling around the pond towards him.

Billy got to his feet and began to run but, within yards, all his breath was gone and he sank to the ground. With his face pressed into the sodden soil he heard him approach; his feet dragging across the twig ridden earth. Billy pushed his arms into the soil but could not raise himself. He shut his eyes and felt his head swim.

Billy opened his eyes to the angry sky as it came in and out of focus. An earthy smell caught his nose; it took a few moments to realise the deep rasping breathing was his own. He must have passed out as he had no memory of being scooped up and carried. He didn't struggle or want to run, but instead he felt his head bob back and forth as the Veteran's arms supported his shoulders and knees. He welcomed the rest and let his breathing fall into step with the rhythmic stumbles of his saviour. He looked into the man's face: the beard, long and unkempt, covered a rigid expression with the eyes fixed at different angles. A battered army cap was rammed on a mass of greying hair and the teeth were yellow, buckled or missing.

When they stopped Billy looked around. He saw the sentry box and the sentry stepping forward from his post. "What 'ave we got 'ere?"

The Veteran did not reply but laid him on the ground, and turned back the way they'd come. Billy wished he'd stay.

"You done well," called the sentry, "I'll mention you in dispatches." He then turned towards Billy. "You all right?" he asked, his mouth moving amongst his laughter lines.

Billy whispered his asthma was bad.

"You passed me earlier," said the soldier, "I thought you was ill."

"I missed the school bus," he replied, but the words came out as a pant, and Billy felt his chest tighten and he could speak no more.

The sentry returned to his post and wound the handle on a field telephone and summoned an ambulance saying a boy had walked past and collapsed.

"When the ambulance comes don't mention that fellow," said the sentry, "'e don't mean no harm but others think 'e do. I 'as a little game with 'im, pretends the war is still on. With all the bumps and bangs of the army up 'ere, 'e believes me."

*

Both the soldier and Billy looked towards the forbidden track. From around a bend, obscured by a clump of trees, the ambulance appeared, dragging a cloud of dust behind it.

As it pulled up the engine rattled to a halt, and Billy smelt a strong waft of hot oil. Its number plate was A3079, and he began to chant the number to himself: he feared writing it in his notebook would bring scorn on his illness.

The windscreen was in two sections and peered over the long bonnet like a bespectacled schoolmaster. The mudguards were black and covered in dust. Red crosses were painted on its sides. A nurse appeared from the back, two army stretcher bearers jogged round and dropped a canvas stretcher next to him.

The nurse felt his pulse then his forehead. "We'll take him straight to Devizes."

The inside of the ambulance was stark and hot and the journey rough. The nurse asked him questions and said she didn't get many asthma cases. And Billy chanted A3079 to himself.

As the ambulance set off she made a note of his name and then smiled at him as she put her notebook to one side. He noticed her green eyes, chestnut coloured hair and high cheek bones. He noticed her grey tunic had a wide collar that overlapped a red cape. He noticed how pretty she was.

"Why do you wear that funny hat?" he asked.

"To keep my hair in place, and it's not a funny hat." But she smiled and Billy knew he was not in trouble.

They fell silent until the ambulance slowed and he could hear the noises of the town. "How big's the engine?" he asked as the driver changed down a gear.

The nurse didn't know.

"Have you ever gone really fast in it?"

She had once, when a soldier

had been badly injured in a training exercise.

The ambulance pulled to a halt. "Here we are," she said.

"Will you be staying at the hospital?" he asked.

She wouldn't, and Billy felt his eyes prick with tears.

He was lifted off the stretcher onto a trolley, and the nurse squeezed his hand goodbye. He wished she could stay with him. He was wheeled into a corridor and left alone, he pulled out his notebook and wrote down A3079. He slipped the notebook back into his pocket before an older nurse, with an even bigger hat, leaned over him. "We'll put you in the children's ward, and a doctor will see you shortly."

He was wheeled into a ward and lifted onto a bed. The sheets were firm and crisp but the mattress was thin and the metal rungs pressed into his back. The windows were tall and arched with fanlights which leaned into the room.

He took short breaths to try and build his strength. The aches in his legs eased, but he felt tired and closed his eyes.

*

Billy woke and listened to distant voices from the corridor. A wheel squeaked on a trolley and the smell of disinfectant hung in his nose.

He kept his eyes closed until he heard his name spoken. "Billy, I'm Doctor Williams. I'm going to listen to your chest."

The doctor, a silver-haired man in a white coat with a stethoscope hung about his neck, stood to his left. His mother and father stood at the end of the bed.

"I hear you've had an adventure today," said the doctor.

Billy said nothing.

"It was lucky the soldier found you."

The doctor unbuttoned Billy's shirt, and he felt the cold of the stethoscope against his skin. "Big breath in now."

Billy took a breath.

"Hold it while I count to

three. One, two and three. Now breathe out slowly and cough for me."

Billy breathed out and coughed.

"When did your asthma start?"

"I woke with it," replied Billy.

"Why didn't you stay home?" asked the doctor.

"He didn't tell me he had asthma," interrupted his mother.

*But you knew*, thought Billy. But he did not say anything: it would be 'answering back'.

"You must tell your mother when you get an attack," said the doctor.

"Yes, you must," she added

quickly, glancing briefly towards her husband. "You'd have saved the soldier, the ambulance and the doctor a lot of trouble."

Billy said nothing, his mother always put the blame on him, and if he stood up for himself now she'd only punish him later. Instead he took short, wheezy breaths.

The doctor called a nurse over, passed her two tablets and said, "Give him these and be ready with a bowl."

She collected a glass of water and a yellow enamelled bowl from a table at the end of the ward. Billy looked at the two round orange tablets on the nurse's palm: they would make him sick, like the last

time. The doctors always said it'd
take the asthma away. It never did.
The nurse placed them on his
tongue, offered him the glass of
water and told him to swallow. She
hovered with the bowl. He began
to feel queasy, he knew he was
going to be sick and hated the wait.

He coughed and kecked but
nothing happened though the
nurse put a hand behind his head
and held the bowl to his chin.

The first heave tightened his
chest, the second and third sent a
pain down his breast bone. His
mouth tasted the acid of his vomit,
and he took short pants as he felt
sweat run down his forehead. The
nurse wiped his mouth, covered
the bowl with a white towel and

carried it away.

"Why didn't you go to school?" asked his mother.

"I missed the bus."

"You shouldn't've gone up on the plain," said his father.

The double doors to the ward were open. One of the police sergeants from Devizes, a man with a thin face and large moustache, was talking to a nurse. Billy sensed his father was about to be called away. He watched him beckoned over, watched them talk with no sound, watched him return and whisper in his mother's ear then watched him leave.

"Where's Dad gone?" he whispered.

"Never you mind."

Billy wished his mother would go. A child opposite cried, nurses tended to the beds, pulled screens around and then pulled them back again. His mother was brought a cup of tea and him a beaker of water. He didn't want to sip from the spout, he felt it baby like but his mother insisted.

A clock above the double doors ticked painfully by as she sat glowering at him and, when everybody was out of earshot, she reminded him of what a nuisance and expense he'd caused for one and all. He closed his eyes and pretended to be asleep until the nurse returned and explained it was four o'clock and it was time for her to leave.

After his mother left the nurse brought him a piece of buttered bread, two slices of ham and a chopped up apple. They were spread out on a pale blue plate sat on a wooden tray. She topped up his beaker of water, smiled and then left him.

At six o'clock visitors began to arrive. Billy's stomach clenched with fear that his mother would come back. He closed his eyes and pretended to be asleep again, but all the while he listened intently for her footsteps or voice.

When somebody did approach his bed it wasn't his mother's footsteps he heard. Nor, for that matter, was it his father's. Whoever it was did not speak, instead a smell of burnt coal teased his nose.

Billy opened his eyes. It was Uncle Joe. He pulled up a chair next to the bed, took off his black cap and rested it in the lap of his blue overalls.

Billy smiled and his uncle smiled back.

"I saw yer father get off the train. In an 'urry 'e was. But 'e had just enough time to say you'd been found up on the plain and was in the 'ospital with your asthma. So I came to see you." His eyes then flicked mischievously. "Skiving off were 'e?"

Billy shook his head and whispered he'd missed the bus.

Uncle Joe nodded and, deep

in thought, fiddled with his hands. It was awhile before he spoke again. "Well you comes and sees me in the future if you misses that bus. I'll get you to school somehow." He then lowered his voice, "And if you don't want to go to school, or just want to be away from 'ome for a bit you come and see me anyway. Any troubles you have you comes and sees me."

This was the most his uncle had ever spoken to him. Billy nodded and Uncle Joe's face relaxed. He took a sixpence from a pocket in his blue overalls and pressed it into Billy's hand.

After Uncle Joe left the doctor listened to his chest again and said they'd try steam. A nurse led him to a bathroom where a tap was thundering hot water into an iron bath. The plug was not in, the bath was part full and steam billowed across the room. A wooden stool was fetched and the nurse pointed to it and Billy sat down.

"Take deep breaths," she said.

Billy tried. He knew this was no good, but he said it helped so he could get back to his bed.

# 3

Billy had a tale to tell. He'd been off school, been in hospital and been discharged on the third afternoon. And now he had walked to Devizes Market Place to catch the school bus home.

Billy felt important.

A group of boys were gathered around a lorry that had pulled to a halt in the market place. Its wheels were held onto its hubs by a circle of large bolts, the boys counted them and then called out the number to a group of girls that stood nearby. The girls giggled and Billy knew they were more interested in the boys than the number of bolts.

Billy's shoulders sagged when he realised nobody cared where he'd been, why he'd not been in school. Instead the other children were more interested in Mike Hillier, who stood alone and aloof.

Another lorry rumbled to a halt and the pack of boys moved over to it, stared the driver out until he walked off and the counting could begin. Billy stood alone, inspecting one of the rear wheels. He counted twelve bolts, took out his notebook and recorded the figure along with the lorry's number plate.

He looked up and saw Paul Redshaw dashing towards him. He tore the notebook from Billy's hands, tossed it to another boy who then kicked it back to Redshaw like it was a football. But Redshaw didn't kick it again, instead he pointed and yelled, "There he is."

Billy's eyes followed Redshaw's outstretched arm. The Veteran was hobbling along the edge of the market place, his greatcoat flapping about his knees and his battered army cap tipped forward over his eyes.

"Where is she? Where is she?" taunted the children.

Billy asked a girl what they meant.

"Molly Hillier, stupid," she replied.

"What about her?" asked

Billy.

"She's disappeared."

"And the Veteran took her," replied another.

With Paul Redshaw distracted, Billy grabbed his notebook and ran to the market cross and sat on the stone steps away from the boys. His chest felt tight as he watched the Veteran listen to the taunts. He thought of Molly, her long dark locks, her freckles and how she always smiled at him. He didn't believe the Veteran would have taken her.

The bus arrived, Billy got to his feet and watched Mike Hillier board. He had to wait, to wait for Redshaw to be out of the way before timing his run from the market cross to the bus.

But Redshaw didn't move and the bus doors began to close. Billy started his run then sank to the ground as his chest tightened. He heard the driver engage the gearbox, heard the noise of the engine pick up and heard the tyres pull forward on the cobbles of the market place. And, as the bus passed by, the girls and boys pointed from the windows and laughed at him lying on the ground.

Billy shut his eyes and took short breaths then felt himself rise in the air: he smelt the same earthy smell as on the plain. Recognising the Veteran's coat, he opened his eyes as he was carried the short distance back to the market cross. He was parked down on the steps to rest, and the Veteran sat next to him.

"They think you took Molly Hillier."

The Veteran turned to Billy, his eyes looked frightened. He shook his head back and forth by no more than an inch at a time. He dug deep in his overcoat and pulled out an apple and offered it. Billy took it, crunched into it. It was a wild apple with a bitter taste. Billy ate it, afraid if he did not the Veteran might think he believed the catcalls of the children.

"They'll get you if the grownups believe them," said Billy.

The Veteran said nothing

but sat with his eyes angled towards Billy.

"You need to hide."

The Veteran pointed to his mouth and shook his head.

"I'll leave food for you. At the dew pond," said Billy, before realising the debt of his promise.

The Veteran nodded, then got to his feet and shuffled away.

*

Billy woke to his father's voice: "You missed the bus?" He looked up from where he was still sat on the steps of the market cross. His father was in uniform.

"Tom Wilkins was on foot patrol this afternoon. He sent word

that you were here. I've got a taxi.
You've been here a few hours
haven't you?"

Billy did not respond.

"Come on."

Billy knew his father never
got too cross with him when he'd
been sick. Instead he took his hand
and led him across the market
place, passing stall holders setting
up their tables where tomorrow
they'd be busy undercutting the
shops, and the shops would close
for half a day.

The taxi was a deep blue
Austin with spoked wheels, black
wings and a black roof. He'd seen it
before, had collected its number so
there was no need to write it down
again.

Billy's father helped him in to the back then slid in to the seat beside him.

The driver checked his mirror then pulled the car forward, crunching his way through the gears. "You looking for that Molly Hillier?"

His father remained tight lipped.

"She set off for school and never arrived they say." Billy's father did not flinch and the driver checked his mirror again. "Pretty girl that Molly Hillier. Some says it's that Veteran fellow that's taken her."

"Who says?" asked Billy's father.

"Just some that says." And

the driver smiled, clearly pleased that his digging and teasing for a titbit of information had worked.

"Well some that says should mind their business."

"Just saying," said the driver.

"I can't arrest a man without evidence."

"'e were seen on the plain carrying a child. Limp they says."

"What day?" asked his father.

"The day she went missing."

Billy realised that it was he that the Veteran had been seen carrying, but he did not mention it as he did not want to add fuel to the story that the Veteran had been in the village on the day Molly Hillier went missing.

Billy's father turned his head to the driver and the driver turned and smiled.

"Who says?"

"I 'ears things," replied the driver.

"But you don't know the person who saw this?"

The driver did not answer.

"If I acted on everything I was told that was seen by people unknown I'd never get a moment's rest," sighed his father.

"I saw Reg Quinnell carrying a sack up the plain road," said Billy. "Across his shoulders."

"Reg Quinnell works over Patney way," said his father, "couldn't be him."

"And Reg Quinnell is Molly

Hillier's uncle," said the driver, "couldn't've been him. I expect it was that Veteran you saw."

"No, it was Reg Quinnell," said Billy.

"Don't make up lies about Quinnell," said his father, "the man's got enough trouble comforting his sister."

"He's a good man," said the driver then looked to Billy's father who nodded, and the driver smiled.

The sun turned the fields golden between Devizes and Market Lavington and the trees cast long shadows as birds made diving swoops with their bellies glowing in the sun.

The taxi laboured its way

over Monument Hill, the driver dropping through the gears until it reached the brow where it sped up as it headed down towards Market Lavington.

The brakes made a short squeal as the driver pulled up outside the house. His father paid the driver as Billy got out. His mother opened the door and demanded, "Why weren't you on the bus?"

"I missed it," said Billy, stepping from the taxi then walking past her.

"Salute your grandfather."

Billy turned towards the photograph on the dresser and did as he was told, but the salute was brief.

She turned towards his father. "Did you get him to blow your whistle?"

Billy always dreaded this; to appease his mother, and to prove his asthma had gone, he had to sound a note on his father's police whistle.

"No," replied his father, stepping into the kitchen.

"Give it to me," her voice was angry yet weary.

Billy's father pulled his whistle from a pocket in his tunic and handed it to her. She wiped the mouth piece on her apron then handed it to Billy.

Billy had done this before, knew he had to get a short shrill to appease his mother. He breathed in until his chest hurt, raised the silver cylinder, clamped his lips around the mouthpiece and blew quickly and sharply.

It gave a short, sharp shrill.

"All right, all right, no need to wake the dead."

\*

Billy laid on his bed and listened to the grumbles of his mother, and the pacifications of his father, waft, with the smell of dinner, up the stairs.

He jumped to a rat-a-tat-tat on the door knocker. It was somebody for his father. Visitors were rare, but his mother always put on the pleasant face that she kept by the door for them. He heard her explaining she had Billy upstairs sick and just out of hospital. The caller gave her sympathy that he felt should be his alone and Billy felt his breath tighten in his chest again. He clenched his fists, thought for a moment then swung his legs off his bed and made his way downstairs and opened the door to the kitchen.

The caller looked surprised to see him and his mother's face darkened. He knew she'd be angry with him again, but it was worth it to show the visitor that he was not the burden she was making him out to be.

"Say good evening to Mr

Baker," she said.

"Good evening."

Billy watched his mother's eyes flash towards his father.

His father did nothing.

"Address Mr Baker as Mr Baker," she added.

"Sorry, Mr Baker."

"That's all right, Billy," replied the man, smiling through a set of uneven, yellowing teeth. "Are you better now?"

"Yes, thank you," he replied.

"Good," said his father, "you can nip down to Nettleton's then and get me some matches and papers."

Billy turned to his mother. "Can I get you any shopping?" He watched her eyes, waiting for her response, hoping he'd done enough to show that he was not as ill as she was trying to make out.

"That won't be necessary," she replied curtly. "Mind you come straight back and rest in your room afterwards." Her eyes, black with anger, darted from side to side.

Billy smiled to himself as he slipped out of the door. He needed no further excuse.

He made his way to Nettleton's store. The sun was starting to dip, the shadows were growing and the trees were whispering as if they knew the guilty plan upon his mind.

The store was empty of customers, it always was around supper time. The women had finished their shopping hours before and the children, sent to fetch things the women had forgotten, were now at home eating their meals.

"Hello Billy," said Mr Nettleton from behind the counter. "Are you feeling better?"

Billy nodded.

"Do you have a list for me?"

Billy shook his head and a silence fell between them.

"Can you remember what your mother sent you for?"

Billy paused, sure that Mr Nettleton could read the guilt on his face. But his voice was kind, and his eyes were smiling. "Matches," he began, "and papers."

Mr Nettleton reached behind

him, took a box of Swan Vestas and a packet of Rizlas from a shelf and put them on the glass counter in front of Billy. He then looked enquiringly in case there was anything else.

"And," said Billy, his eyes settling on a round china tray with a glass dome cover, "two of those pork pies." He felt his breathing go tight, and he was sure his face had turned a bright shade of red.

Mr Nettleton lifted the lid, selected two pies and then wrapped them in grease proof paper. "Anything else?"

Billy shook his head.

"On your mother's account?"

Billy nodded and, as Mr

Nettleton opened a ledger and turned the pages, Billy pulled the shopping towards him and slipped out of the shop.

*

Billy's parents, Mr Baker, and another man barely noticed him come back from Nettleton's store. He placed his father's Rizlas and matches on the dresser before he slipped upstairs, sat on the edge of his bed and stared down at the two pork pies he'd smuggled in beneath his jumper.

The pies had a hard golden brown pastry crust: Mr Nettleton's pies were always good and he hoped the Veteran would like them. But with that thought a wave of foreboding fear swept up through him: he still had to get out of the house unseen, get to the dew pond and hide them.

He thought about not going, ignoring his commitment. But the Veteran had saved him and now it was his turn to save the Veteran: the promise he'd made was a debt unpaid.

He heard other men arrive and with each man arrived a morsel of news about the Veteran. He'd been seen late afternoon on the Devizes Road. He'd been seen crossing the fields towards Market Lavington, and he'd been seen on the road up to the plain. He froze when he heard Reg Quinnell, loud and forthright, remind everybody that was where he'd been seen carrying a child on the day his niece had gone missing.

"He's gone to mess with her body," said another.

"Fred!" said Billy's mother, her voice full of scolding anger.

Billy listened intently for Uncle Joe's voice. He didn't want him to be part of this, didn't want him to betray the Veteran.

He looked down at the pies again. There was no call from his mother to come down for supper – he was sure she knew he had them but wasn't letting on.

He reached down and crumbled off a piece of crust. He dropped it on his tongue: the rich, savoury flavours erupted in his dry mouth, and his stomach panged for more.

Another man arrived, he feared it would be Mr Nettleton to ask if they'd enjoyed the pies. But no, it was a voice he didn't recognise: a man who willingly joined in with the vitriol against the Veteran.

Then his father's voice was clear and loud. The other voices tailed off and his father spoke with certainty. "It'll be dark soon. I'll go to the army and get some flares. You all go to the sentry post and wait for me there. We'll flush him out and flush him out tonight."

There was a murmur of agreement then his father added,

"Joan, you go to the Telephone Exchange and get them to telephone through to Devizes for more men."

Billy listened as the kitchen emptied, relieved he'd not heard Uncle Joe's voice. He wrapped the pies back up in the greaseproof paper, crossed to his door, opened it and stepped onto the landing. He stopped and listened. There was not a sound from downstairs. He took each step until he reached the door to the kitchen. He opened it gingerly and peered in. It was deserted. He crossed to the dresser, his father's Rizlas and matches were still there. He lifted the lid off the pot where his mother kept the housekeeping money. There were a few half-crowns, a few shillings and some pennies. He looked at his grandfather's photograph, the cap he wore was like the Veteran's. He looked into his grandfather's eyes, but there was no sign of disapproval. He pocketed all the coins: the Veteran would need them to get the last train from Patney.

As he left he made sure all the doors were shut – his bedroom, the stairs and the kitchen door. He scampered along the lanes, avoiding his mother's path back from the Telephone Exchange. The darkness gathered in, and the trees guarding the lanes swayed in the breeze and whispered stories of his deceit.

He cut steeply up the hill to the plain, walking through fields of cows who stopped their munching and stared at him as if they knew where he was going, knew what he had stuffed inside his jumper and knew he would be caught.

He reached the track beyond the sentry post. He could hear the men gathering. And the men had brought their dogs, and when one began to bark the others followed suit until the night air was filled with the sound of a howling pack. And when the men had managed to quieten their dogs, distant barks from distant farms and hamlets, echoed back as other dogs answered as dogs are prone to do.

He hurried to the dew pond

where, amongst the trees leaning towards the water which reflected the light of a rising moon, was the Veteran. He was going from tree to tree, from bush to bush, searching for the promised cache of food.

"Veteran," whispered Billy. The man froze, his body rigid. "It's me, Billy." And with that he hurried over to the man and pulled the pies from beneath his jumper.

The Veteran took them and his hands trembled as he pulled away the paper wrapper. He rewrapped one and pocketed it in his greatcoat. The other he held in both hands and rammed it into his mouth. Billy could hear his teeth grating as they yanked chunks off the pie. The meat smelt sweet and fresh and Billy's stomach rumbled with his own hunger.

"They're after you. They think you took Molly Hillier," said Billy.

The Veteran stopped his eating for a moment and stared at the boy and Billy saw the same fright he'd seen in those eyes in Devizes Market Place.

"I've brought you money, you need to get the train from Patney. The last one goes to Newbury."

Billy didn't know where Newbury was but he knew the timetables: the stations to the east, the stations to the west. He knew the times but did not know the places. But Newbury was in bold type on those timetables so it must be big – he was sure that the Veteran could hide there and find someone to help him.

The Veteran stuffed the last of the pie into his mouth and swallowed. The dogs barked again but this time not so far in the distance.

"Come on," said Billy. He tugged at the man's greatcoat and he followed him back onto the track. They took a path, a steep path, from the track, down the embankment of the plain to a lane that led to the railway cutting. And all the time the sound of the barking dogs grew louder.

Billy feeling fearful, raised his hand and the Veteran took it in his giant, rough paw as they fell in step.

Billy slid down the railway bank, dragging the Veteran's arm behind him. Earth crept into his shoes as his ankles twisted against the rough terrain.

"We won't scramble up t'other bank," said Billy, "we'll walk along the rails."

Billy felt the stone ballast against the thin soles of his shoes. The Veteran let go his hand and stopped.

"We've got to get to Patney," said Billy.

The church bells began to strike. Billy counted the strikes. He knew there'd be ten but he counted them all the same.

"We've seven minutes," he said.

He stepped on the iron rail, then on to the wooden sleepers. The Veteran followed him. They passed where the line branched to Devizes and stumbled on towards Patney.

Billy heard a slight buzz, a slight tingle from the track. It grew to a ringing then the noise of the train itself filled the air. It came from behind. "It's your train," he told the Veteran.

The noise of the train grew and Billy quickened their pace, and the Veteran stumbled on the stone ballast and on the sleepers, between the rails, as he fought against his gait. Then the sky exploded in light as the fireball of a flare rose in the sky above Patney. The Veteran was no longer a shadow, a silhouette or a presence made by grunts and mumbles. Now he was a figure, a fully lit figure. His eyes shone and his greatcoat took on its khaki colour and the grass of the banks was green, the hawthorn bushes brown and the rabbit burrows spewed their sandy soil. And the rails glistened as two silver streaks paving the way ahead.

Billy stepped off the line but the Veteran froze between the rails. The noise of the train grew until it was no longer a cacophony of sounds: the wheels could be heard spinning against the rails, the carriages were now clanking behind, and the steam engine drove the pistons with a rhythmic thud.

The Veteran sank to his knees and, with his body between the rails, covered his head and quivered.

"Get off the line," yelled Billy.

The column of smoke marked the bend behind them. The train's whistle filled the air and the note of the engine changed as it slowed for Patney. And the rails began to vibrate and Billy could not hear himself when he shouted again.

Billy stepped over the rail, back onto the line and tugged at the back of the Veteran's coat. To his relief he began to stand, but then he turned to face the train as it came in to view.

The Veteran raised an arm to shield his eyes from the glare of the train's main headlight. Billy tugged harder at his coat as he sank back to his knees. The train's whistle let out a series of short blasts.

Billy pulled at the coat again but the material slipped through his fingers and he fell back onto the line. He scrambled to his feet and, as the noise became deafening, he stepped off the track and felt the rush of wind batter his face and whip at his hair as the train raced by. The air filled with the smell of soot and hot clinker, and when it had passed the Veteran no longer twitched or mumbled. He lay smashed and motionless between the rails, his greatcoat half torn off him, and blood trickled from a deep wound to his forehead. As the flare burnt itself out the cutting fell back in to shadow, and hid the Veteran from his eyes.

Billy's legs trembled and he felt terribly cold. He stared at the spot where the Veteran lay. He tried to speak but no words would come from his throat.

The sound of the engine died as it pulled to a halt in Patney. And still Billy stood and stared, but he knew his friend would never emerge from the darkness.

There were shouts from the station and those shouts turned to men walking up the line and the men walking up the line turned to flashes of tilley lamps and the barking of dogs growing closer.

He didn't want to leave his friend, didn't want his father and the posse of men to be the ones to discover him. He pictured the men standing around, gazing upon the body and muttering their words of blame and hate for taking Molly Hiller. He thought of staying and protesting his friend's innocence, but Reg Quinnell would be among those men and Billy feared he would then know they shared a secret.

He turned and began the

walk back towards Market Lavington, leaving the men to their quarry. As he walked he thought of his uncle Joe. Thought of his blackened hands and his understanding smile. Uncle Joe would believe him. Uncle Joe would know what to do. Billy remembered his promise in the hospital and quickened his pace. He wouldn't go home, he'd go to Uncle Joe's cottage.

And the moon slipped out from behind a cloud and the rabbits stuck their heads from their burrows and nibbled on the fresh night grass.

## Acknowledgements

Many thanks to Suzanne Bellenger, Steven Hampton, Jon Stock and Debz Hobbs-Wyatt who gave me much valued feedback during the development of this work.

## Can you spare some time to give me a review?

Your honest opinion matters to me and will help me gain further sales. You can rate this book on www.amazon.co.uk or www.goodreads.com

Many thanks.
Stephen P. Smith

Printed in Poland
by Amazon Fulfillment
Poland Sp. z o.o., Wrocław